Princesses

For my family, *pétomanes tous* - PB

To Barbara, Lauren & Imogen and
to the rest of my family and friends - EH

SIMON & SCHUSTER
First published in Great Britain in 2019 by Simon & Schuster UK Ltd
1st Floor, 222 Gray's Inn Road, London, WC1X 8HB • A CBS Company
Text copyright © 2019 Peter Bently • Illustrations copyright © 2019 Eric Heyman
The right of Peter Bently and Eric Heyman to be identified as the author and illustrator of this
work has been asserted by them in accordance with the Copyright, Designs and Patents Act, 1988
All rights reserved, including the right of reproduction in whole or in part in any form
A CIP catalogue record for this book is available from the British Library upon request
978-1-4711-6412-5 (PB) • 978-1-4711-6413-2 (eBook)
Printed in China • 10 9 8 7 6 5 4 3 2 1

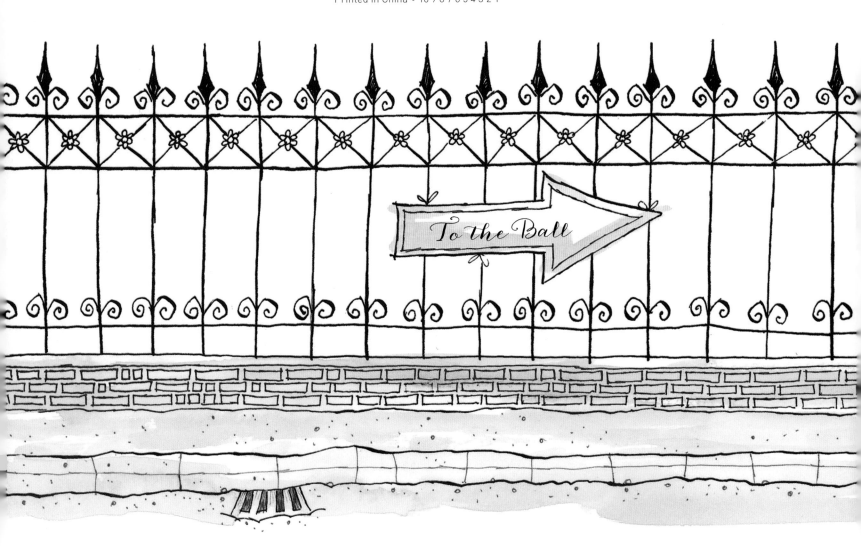

Princesses DON'T PARP!

Peter Bently
&
Eric Heyman

SIMON & SCHUSTER

London   New York   Sydney   Toronto   New Delhi

"Tonight," said the princess, "I'm having a ball.
It's going to be fun! I'm not nervous at all.

There's only one thing that could go a bit wrong -
The King of Pum Ping will be coming along

And everyone here is a parper, you see.
(Princesses don't parp, so I don't include me.)"

Said the princess, "I live in a palace of pooters. Wherever I go there are rear-end-tooters.

The butler does squeaks that he hides with a cough.

The cook makes a noise like a gun going off.

SQUEAK

BANG

And when Peggy, my chambermaid, picks up a pin

She **always** lets off. She just can't keep it in.

The troops on parade are too trumpy to mention -
They all parp at once when they stand to attention!

But the King of Pum Ping won't hear parping from me -
Princesses don't parp, as I'm sure you'll agree.

When Chivers is cranking the car to go shopping
It isn't the engine that makes a loud popping.

POP
POP
POP

Constable Coggins will try to pretend
That you've just heard some fireworks
and not his rear end.

WHIZZ

WHEF

CRACK

FIZZ

BOOOOM

And the constable's baby might *look* very small
But its blasters are some of the biggest of all.

When Madame de Pom Pom sits down with her harp
She simply can't help letting out a loud parp.
It sounds like the air from an untied balloon
And - this is the weird thing - it's always in tune!

MEEEEEEP

And then there's the gardener, old Mr Giles,
Whose parps are so loud you can hear them for miles.
And as for the Reverend Archibald Smedley -
His stinkers are silent but ever so deadly.

I hope all those parpers keep well out of sight
I don't want them pooping my party tonight!

You'd think my relations would silence their rumps
But no! They do some of the very *worst* trumps.

Aunt Carolina sounds just like a frog.
The Duke of Cucumberland startles the dog.

But I'd *never* make Rover run out of the door -
Princesses don't parp, as I told you before.

So when Uncle Edmund asks, 'Who made that pong?
Was it the princess?' - you know he's quite wrong.
It was probably Edmund himself. Or the cat.
Princesses DON'T PARP. It's as simple as that."

As she pulled on her ball dress - the seventh she'd tried -
The princess looked into her mirror and sighed.

"No, you'll never catch *me* doing
bum-blasts or toots.
I do not do bottom-burps,
whizzpops or poots.

That parp in the pews?
It just couldn't be me.

That pump in the pool?
That was someone else, see?

Who whiffed in the lift?
Who rattled the china?

Blame one of the footmen.
Or Aunt Carolina."

"Right," said the princess. "It's time for the ball.
I'm a teensy bit nervous tonight after all!
I *hope* no one parps! They're a windy old bunch.
Thank goodness we didn't have curry for lunch!

It's the king of Pum Ping!

Does my hair look all right?
I mustn't forget to be nice and polite."

The king walked towards her.
Her legs were like jelly.

She felt something weird going on in her belly . . .

A hubbling, bubbling, gurgling and grumbling,
A fluttering, muttering, rolling and rumbling . . .

"Oh no!" thought the princess.
"It cannot be true.
It's all this excitement!
It simply won't do!

Princesses *don't* parp! I *can't* let off now!
But the King of Pum Ping is beginning to bow

So I've really no choice. I must welcome my guest.
I'll just have to curtsey and hope for the best!"

PAARRPPPPPPPPP!

"I'm sorry!" she cried. "What an awful disgrace!"

The king had a very shocked look on his face.

"But why are you sorry, Princess?" asked the king.
"That's just how we all say hello in Pum Ping!
We do not shake hands and say, 'How do you do?'
We bow and we PARP very loudly, like you!"

PAAAARRRRRPPPPP!!!!

The princess said, "Right! Let the party begin!
Let's be like our guests - and don't keep it IN!"

They parped through the night till the sun rose at last
And one thing's for certain . . .

they all had a BLAST!